"That guy's not a delivery man!"

"He's a thief! He's stealing our pizza money!" Salem gasped.

"You've go to stop him!" Stonehenge whispered back.

"Right, I—" Salem looked at the hamster. "What do you mean, *I've* got to stop him?"

Stonehenge rolled his eyes. "What do I look like? A pit bull?"

"But confronting crooks makes me break out in a rash," Salem whined.

Before they could decide what to do, Stonehenge peeked out again. "Sabrina's going to kill you," he squeaked.

Salem peeked out through the crack.

He saw the thief stick his hand under Sabrina's mattress, then head for the door.

In his hand was Sabrina's enchanted locket!

Sabrina, The Teenage Witch™
Salem's Tails™

#1 Cat TV
#2 Teacher's Pet
  Salem Goes to Rome (tie-in)

Available from MINSTREL Books

SALEM GOES TO ROME

Written by Cathy East Dubowski and Mark Dubowski
Based upon the television movie
written by Daniel Berendsen

Based on Characters Appearing in Archie Comics

And based upon the television series
Sabrina, The Teenage Witch
Created for television by Nell Scovell
Developed for television by Jonathan Schmock

A
MINSTREL®
BOOK

Published by POCKET BOOKS
New York   London   Toronto   Sydney   Tokyo   Singapore

A MINSTREL PAPERBACK *Original*

 A Minstrel Book published by
POCKET BOOKS, a division of Simon & Schuster Inc.
1230 Avenue of the Americas, New York, NY 10020

ISBN: 0-671-02773-5

First Minstrel Books printing October 1998

10 9 8 7 6 5 4 3 2 1

A MINSTREL PAPERBACK and colophon are registered trademarks of Simon & Schuster Inc.

SABRINA THE TEENAGE WITCH and all related titles, logos
and characters are trademarks of Archie Comics Publications, Inc.

Printed in the U.S.A.

Prologue

It all begin when Sabrina Spellman's father, Edward, gave her an antique gold locket. It had once belonged to a beautiful young witch named Sophia. She fell in love with a mortal artist named Roberto, but he betrayed her and told her secret. So she lost her powers, which were then trapped inside the locket.

For four centuries everyone in the Spellman family had tried to open the locket. But all had failed. In two weeks its magic would be lost forever. Sabrina's family sent her to Italy to find the answer and release the power trapped within.

But when she got to Rome, Sabrina discovered she was not alone. Her cat—

1

Salem Saberhagen—had stowed away on the plane.

Now they were staying in a small hotel run by Signora Guadagno, a witch who had lost her powers, and her son, Alberto. Sabrina's roommate was a young witch from England named Gwen. Instead of a cat, she had a hamster, Stonehenge. Just like Salem, Stonehenge was being punished by the Witches' Council for misbehavior. Salem knew it must have been something really bad for them to make him a hamster!

Chapter 1

"So much pasta—so little time!"

It was Salem the cat's first trip to Rome, Italy. It was dinnertime. And he'd read in the guidebook that there were more than thirty different kinds of pasta to try. He couldn't wait to get started.

He sprang across the hotel room toward Sabrina Spellman's open backpack. "Gotta go!" he said, using one of Sabrina's favorite expressions.

"FREEZE!" Sabrina cried as she pointed her index finger at the startled black cat.

Frosty sparkles showered across the room.

Salem froze mid-leap five feet in the air. He looked like a party balloon without the string.

It isn't easy living with a teenage witch, Salem thought with a sigh. Especially for Salem. He hadn't always been a cat. He'd once been a powerful warlock. But then he got in trouble with the Witches' Council. *Hey, I only tried to take over the world!* Salem thought.

As punishment, the Witches' Council turned him into a cat for a hundred years. A cat with no powers.

Well, only one. He could talk.

"Sabrina," he meowed, dangling his paws in the air. "Do you mind?"

Sabrina stood nose to nose with her talking cat. "First, tell me where you thought you were going."

"With you, of course," Salem replied. "To some fabulous Italian restaurant, where I will pig out on pasta until I practically explode . . ."

"Eeww," Sabrina said.

"It's just a figure of speech, Sabrina."

"Well, sorry to disappoint you, Salem,"

4

Sabrina said. "But you're staying home tonight."

"*What?!*"

Sabrina chose that exact moment to release her spell.

Salem fell—*oww!*—and landed on his behind.

He definitely needed a checkup. Weren't cats always supposed to land on their feet?

"Take me with you," he begged, which was rare for Salem. He tried to look pitiful. "*Ple-e-eeeese!*"

"Sorry, Salem." Sabrina scooped him up and dumped him on the bed. "But you're being a real pain in the neck."

"That's not nice," Salem replied.

Sabrina laughed. "I'm sort of teasing you, Salem. But I've been carrying you around Rome in my backpack for two whole days, and it actually is giving me a pain. A real one. In my neck."

Salem sucked in his tummy. "Sorry.

Must have been all the peanuts I ate coming over on the plane. They *are* rather fattening."

Sabrina leaned over to adjust his collar. Signora Guadagno had given him a new ID tag with the address of the hotel, just in case. It was stuck in the buckle. She fixed it for him. "That's okay. But I really need a break. So I thought, well, maybe you might enjoy staying in the room with Stonehenge for the night?"

Salem looked doubtful. "The only place the words *enjoy* and *Stonehenge* belong together is on a recipe card! I wonder how long you should cook hamster?"

Sabrina put her foot down. "Alberto's taking us out to dinner at a *real* Italian restaurant—one that doesn't allow pets. You and Stonehenge are staying here."

"But, Sabrina," Salem whined, "what are we supposed to do all night? There's not even a TV."

"Dinner? Did somebody say dinner?"

Stonehenge the hamster scampered into the room, followed by Gwen.

"Shhh!" Sabrina covered Salem's mouth with her hand. "Look, Salem, you've got to promise to behave yourself while I'm gone."

Salem dropped his head onto his paws and stared at the floor. "Why should I?"

"Because I'll tell Aunt Hilda and Aunt Zelda," Sabrina suggested. "And they'll report you to the Witches' Council if you don't. How's that?"

"That's a good reason," Salem agreed. He sighed and raised his right paw. "I promise."

Stonehenge frowned, but didn't say anything.

"Good." Sabrina looked in the mirror over her dresser and zapped on a few outfits until she found one she liked.

"What do you think?" she asked Gwen.

"Super!" Gwen declared. "Very Italian. Very *bella! Bella!*"

Salem made a noise.

"What?" Sabrina asked.

"Well, if you ask me," Salem began, "I mean, I'm no Valentino, no Armani, no Laura Biagiotti . . ." He went on, naming several famous Italian designers. "But . . ."

"But what?"

"It's the locket," Salem said. "It just doesn't work with the dress, darling."

"You don't have to be so catty."

Sabrina held up the locket. Salem was right. It was too ornate to go with the simple lines of the dress. She unfastened the clasp and removed it from around her neck. "I'll just carry it in my purse."

"Think you should, mate?" Gwen asked. "What if you lose it? What if someone nicks your purse?" Gwen and her hamster were from England. Sometimes Sabrina had to think a minute to translate.

"Steals my purse?" Sabrina thought about it. "Maybe you're right. But do you think it's safe to leave it in the room?"

"Of course, luv," Gwen said. "Especially with two warlocks to guard it."

Sabrina and Gwen looked at the two "warlocks." One black cat with an attitude and a hamster with a really bad overbite. Both totally stripped of their powers, except for the ability to talk, which they tended to abuse, anyway.

The girls burst out laughing.

Salem was *not* amused. "I assure you I am quite capable of looking after a locket," he said. "The rodent, I'm not so sure about."

Stonehenge glared. "Speak for y'self," he said.

"Okay, you two," Sabrina said. "But I think I should hide it, just in case." She looked around the room. "I know!" She hurried to the bed and slipped the locket between the mattress and box spring.

Salem rolled his eyes. "No one would ever think of looking there," he said. He was being sarcastic. Everybody knew that hiding place—especially burglars!

A knock at the door made Sabrina whirl around. But it was just Alberto, Signora Guadagno's eighteen-year-old son. He had agreed to be their tour guide and show them the sights. "Ready for going?" he asked. "I myself am starvation." Alberto was still working on his English.

"You mean starving," Sabrina said helpfully. "Me, too."

Then she turned to her cat. "Now remember, Salem, don't go anywhere. And don't let anyone in the room." She glanced at her British friend, then lowered her voice to a whisper. "And whatever you do, don't eat Stonehenge!"

Salem made a face. "All right. I promise. But would you at least bring me—and I absolutely *hate* this term—a *doggie* bag?"

Sabrina grinned. "You got it."

Sabrina and Gwen set out some cat food and some hamster chow.

"Gotta go!" Sabrina said. And then they were gone.

"I love you, too," Salem muttered.

Stonehenge sighed. Then, with a shrug, he began to nibble the little pellets of hamster food.

But not Salem. He stared down at his bowl with a look of misery.

Then he studied the chubby little hamster.

"What?" Stonehenge asked, looking up. "Do I have hamster food in my teeth?"

"How can you eat that stuff?" Salem asked.

"Well, mate, I just open my mouth and—"

"We deserve better than this," Salem interrupted. He leaped to the balcony and looked down. Salem, Gwen, and Alberto disappeared down the street.

"Excellent!" Salem cried as he leaped to the floor. *"Viva la pízza!"*

11

Chapter 2

Salem! What are you going to do?" Stonehenge asked.

"We may be stuck in this room all night," Salem replied. "But we don't have to settle for dried nuggets of an unknown origin."

With his paw, he batted at the phone till the receiver tumbled off the hook. "I'm ordering a real Italian pizza—cooked in a real wood-burning oven. From a restaurant that delivers, American-style."

Stoney's tiny little eyes lit up. "Veggie supreme?" he asked hopefully.

Salem wrinkled his nose. "I was thinking more along the lines of the meat-lovers' special."

"Veggies!" Stonehenge insisted.

"Meat!"

They argued until Salem's growling stomach told him that any pizza was better than no pizza. So he compromised. Half veggie, half sausage and pepperoni.

"But will they deliver to a cat?" Stonehenge asked.

"Been there, done that," Salem replied smoothly. He quickly dialed the phone.

The pizza restaurant answered. Salem spoke into the phone using his most elegant "human" voice. The voice that almost led a revolution to take over the world. The voice that could get a pizza delivered anywhere he pleased. Maybe.

After a pause he held the phone away from his face. He'd forgotten one tiny detail.

Salem didn't speak Italian!

"Uh, Stonehenge," Salem whispered. "Got any idea what *non capisco* means?"

"Course, matey," Stonehenge said with a laugh. "It means 'I don't understand.' The people at the pizza restaurant must not speak English."

Salem looked horrified. "Now what do I do?"

"Well," Stonehenge said, "in a previous life, I spent half a century in the Italian navy. I still remember a few words. Navy words . . ."

"Stoney! Speak to me!" Salem begged. "Tell me how to order pizza in Italian!"

Stonehenge wrinkled his tiny pink nose. "Maybe. If you say 'pretty please.' "

Salem groaned. He couldn't believe it. Groveling before a rodent! But his stomach argued with him to do whatever it took. So at last he said, "Okay, okay. Pr-pr-pruh . . ." He winced. "P-pretty please?"

"With sugar on top?"

"Just tell me what to say!" Salem growled.

Stonehenge told Salem how to order pizza in Italian. Salem repeated every word into the phone. Then he hung up.

"Wait a minute," Stonehenge said. "Aren't you forgetting something?"

"Oh," Salem said, "did you want a side salad?"

"Actually, that would have been nice," Stonehenge said. "But that's not what I mean. How are you going to answer the door when the pizza bloke arrives?"

"Hmm. Back home Sabrina always answers the door."

"Sabrina's not here, mate," Stonehenge pointed out.

Salem frowned.

"Here's what we'll do, mate," Stonehenge suggested. "Leave the door unlocked. Put a note on it that says bring the pizza inside. And we'll leave the money on the table."

"But what about when he sees that no one's here?" Salem challenged.

"We'll hide in the bathroom with the shower on," Stonehenge said, proud of his quick thinking.

15

Salem thought about it. "Okay," he said. "But I can't believe I'm taking advice from a mouse."

"I'm not a mouse," Stonehenge snapped. "I'm a hamster!"

"Same thing . . ." Salem muttered.

"I heard that!" Stonehenge cried.

Salem counted out some money for the pizza and laid it on the table near the door.

"This better work," Salem said. *Growl!*

"Take it easy," Stonehenge said.

"That wasn't *me* growling," Salem said. "It was my stomach! I'm *starving!*"

The two animals hurried into the bathroom. Salem could hardly wait. His mouth watered as he thought about the crispy crust, the hot, gooey cheese . . .

"Blimey!" Stonehenge complained. "Move over, mate. You're drooling on my head!"

At last they heard footsteps on the stairs.

16

"Quick!" Stonehenge whispered.

Careful not to get wet, Salem pawed the faucet till he turned on the shower.

Then he and Stonehenge crouched near the door to listen.

Salem sniffed the air, then frowned. "That's strange," he whispered to Stonehenge. "I don't smell pizza yet." He rubbed his nose with his paw. "I hope I'm not coming down with a cold."

"Shhhh!" Stonehenge hissed. "He'll hear you!"

A moment later they heard the heavy wooden door to their room cre-e-e-eak slowly open.

Stonehenge jabbed Salem in the ribs. "Go ahead! Tell him what to do!"

"Uh, hello, I—"

"Ciao, signore!" Stonehenge hissed. "It means 'hello, sir!'"

"Oh, yeah—ciao, signore," Salem called out, pretending to be a man in the shower.

17

Then Stonehenge fed him a long string of complicated-sounding Italian words. The words felt strange on Salem's tongue as he repeated them one by one.

"*Grazie,*" the man called out.

Salem knew that meant "thank you." He turned to Stonehenge. "What did I just say?"

"You told him, 'I'm taking a shower. The money is on the table. Leave the pizza, and keep the change.'"

"What?" Salem shrieked. That was a *lot* of change. He stuck his head near the crack in the door. "Uh, wait, signore—" How did you say "Just kidding" in Italian?

But then Salem choked—and not from a hairball. "S-S-Stonehenge!" he whispered. "L-look!"

Stonehenge crawled between Salem's front paws and looked.

The man in the room was dressed all in black, from his shiny pointed shoes to his wide-brimmed hat.

Yes, he was picking up the money off the table.

But he *didn't* have a pizza!

"I knew I didn't smell pepperoni!" Salem whispered to Stonehenge. "Where's our food?"

Cat and hamster watched the man pocket the money. They watched him glance at the bathroom door with a sneaky look in his eyes. Then they watched him tiptoe around the room, as if he were looking for something.

Something to steal!

"Stonehenge, that guy's not a delivery man," Salem gasped. "He's a thief! He's stealing our pizza money!"

"You've got to stop him!" Stonehenge whispered back.

"Right, I—" Salem looked at the hamster. "What do you mean, *I've* got to stop him?"

Stonehenge rolled his eyes. "What do I look like? A pit bull?"

19

"But confronting crooks makes me break out in a rash," Salem whined.

Before they could decide what to do, Stonehenge peeked out again. "Sabrina's going to kill you," he squeaked.

Salem peeked out through the crack.

He saw the thief stick his hand under Sabrina's mattress, then head for the door.

In his hand was Sabrina's enchanted locket!

Chapter 3

Salem felt as if he might swoon. "This is all your fault!" he declared.

"*My* fault?" Stonehenge exclaimed. "Blimey! *You're* the one who thought it would be so clever to pretend to be a human and order pizza!"

"Yeah, but *you're* the one who said to leave the door open with *my* money out on the table," Salem shot back. "You practically invited the thief into our room, you rat—"

"Hamster! Hamster! I'm a hamster!"

"We'll discuss your family tree later," Salem replied disdainfully. "Right now we've got to go and get that locket!"

"But how?" Stonehenge asked.

"I have no idea," Salem said as he headed for the door. "But I'm sure you'll think of something."

Salem heard the hamster muttering something under his breath. At least he was coming.

"This will be easy," Salem told Stonehenge as they ran down the stairs. "He'll never suspect he's being followed by a cat and mouse." Stonehenge gnashed his teeth at Salem's remark.

But when they reached the front gate, Salem's heart sank.

The thief was climbing into the backseat of a taxi.

"What were you saying about easy?" Stonehenge asked.

"We'll have to run," Salem snapped. "Come on, you can use the exercise."

Stonehenge dug in his heels. "Why should *I* go? Sabrina's not my witch. And the locket's not my problem. I'm going to go back to the room and do what I should have done in the first place. Ignore you. Have some hamster chow. Then turn in with a good book." He turned to go.

Salem's paw clamped down on the little hamster's back.

"*Aiuto!*" the hamster squealed, calling for help. "*Polizia!*"

"Forget it, pal," Salem said. "The police in this town are too busy to waste their time on the problems of two little animals like you and me. Like it or not, we're in this together. You're the reason this guy stole Sabrina's locket. And you're going to help me get it back."

"Why should I?" Stonehenge demanded.

"Because," Salem said, "if we don't get it back, we're both going to be in trouble. Big trouble. The Spellmans will report us to the Witches' Council. And the Witches' Council will probably extend our punishment for another hundred years. They

23

might even turn us into something a whole lot worse than a cat and a hamster."

"Worse?" Stonehenge shuddered. "Like what?"

Salem shrugged. "A cockroach. A slug. An intestinal flu bug. I don't know—and I don't want to find out. Come on!"

"I guess you're right," Stonehenge admitted. "But I don't know if I can keep up . . ."

"Grab on to my tail!" Salem shouted. The taxi was pulling away.

Stonehenge grabbed Salem's tail. Together they scampered down the street.

Luckily it was rush hour. Traffic still clogged the Italian streets. The thief's taxi driver stopped and started, shouting and blowing his horn.

"Couldn't we just buy Sabrina a new bloomin' locket?" Stonehenge gasped when the taxi paused for a light at the corner. "This running is wearing me out."

"Maybe," Salem said cattily, "you

24

should actually use that little treadmill Gwen put in your cage once in a while."

"Oh, like you're an Olympic runner?" Stonehenge snapped.

Salem hated to admit it, but he was getting tired, too. Jogging was not his idea of vacation fun. But what else could he do? The stitch in his side was a lot less painful than what Sabrina would do to him if he went home without the locket!

Finally the taxi pulled over to the curb.

"He's getting out," Stonehenge reported.

"Hey!" Salem complained. "I bet that's *my* money he's paying the driver with! And I'll bet he overtips!"

With renewed outrage and energy, Salem ran toward the thief. Stonehenge did his best to keep up.

The man in black took an outdoor seat at a restaurant called Ristorante Bernini. It was named after Rome's most famous sculptor.

It reminded Salem of a café in Westbridge. White tablecloths on little round tables inside a little iron fence in front of a building with a big plate-glass window. There was just one difference.

A couple of stray cats were lounging near the diners.

And the people weren't shooing them away. They were feeding them!

Salem's tummy rumbled. *I never did get that pizza,* he thought. "Um, Stonehenge, you stay behind this mailbox and keep an eye on the suspect. I'll go over and blend in with those other cats. See what I can find out."

Salem hurried toward the restaurant. It was hard to keep his mind on his mission with those tempting smells wafting through the air.

Now, this was Italian that Salem could understand. *Spaghetti. Lasagne. Mozzarella. Garlic bread* . . .

Someone dropped a fried mozzarella ball. Salem pounced.

Ah, this is the life, Salem sighed dreamily.

Eating great food in an outdoor ristorante. Watching the sun set over the Roman skyline.

A pretty white kitty glanced his way.

And mixing with the locals. Salem grinned back. *Bella! Bella!* He started to walk over.

"Psssst!"

Salem glanced back at the noise. Stonehenge glared at him and waved him back.

Oh, yeah, Salem thought. He'd nearly forgotten why he was here.

Reluctantly Salem padded over. The thief was speaking to the waiter. It seemed to Salem as if they knew each other. But Salem couldn't understand a word.

He turned to Stonehenge. "What are they saying?" Salem whispered.

"These two are mates," Stonehenge explained. "The waiter calls him *Il Gatto*—which means 'The Cat.'"

"You mean like 'cat burglar'?"

"The waiter is asking him if he's going

27

to join some friends to play cards, but Il Gatto says no. He has to meet someone."

Just then the thief pulled something from his pocket to show the waiter.

"Sabrina's locket!" Salem gasped.

The thief laid it on the table, then picked up his menu.

"Now's my chance!" Salem whispered. He wound his way around the mailbox. The pretty white kitty came toward him.

Not now, baby, Salem thought. *You might get hurt.* He was already crouched and ready to pounce.

A-choooooo!

Stonehenge sneezed.

Salem and the other cats turned around and stared at him.

Nobody meowed. But Salem and Stonehenge both knew what the other cats were thinking.

They were thinking, *Oh, boy! Dessert! Meowwwwrrrrll!*

Stonehenge took off.

Chapter 4

Salem had two seconds to decide. Look after the locket—or save Stonehenge?

The locket was important because it belonged to Sabrina. It was a gift from her father. And it was why they were in Rome.

Stonehenge belongs to Gwen, Salem reasoned. *He can be quite irritating at times. And he is a rodent.*

The locket was important because it was magical. It was the only one like it in the entire world.

Stonehenge, Salem reminded himself, *is a hamster. And there is another hamster born every sixty seconds.*

If he lost the locket, Sabrina would never forgive him.

If I lose Stonehenge, Salem further reasoned, *Sabrina will never even have to know.*

The locket was Sabrina's. Sabrina, after all, was Salem's friend.

Cats and hamsters, Salem reflected, *are natural enemies.*

Every reason why Salem should *not* help Stonehenge flashed through his mind.

But Salem's paws weren't paying any attention. They were too busy running to the rescue.

Sometimes I'm just too good for my own good, Salem told himself. He skittered around the corner and followed the tails of the other cats up a dark and cluttered alley. A trash can banged as they went by.

One thing was certain in Salem's mind. If he did manage to save Stonehenge, the little hamster would have to promise not to ever tell another soul. Not even Gwen or Sabrina.

A cat saving a hamster. It was humiliating!

By the time Salem's eyes got completely used to the dark, the other cats had already reached the end of the alley and were heading for another street.

Stonehenge, out in front, faked a left and went right.

He's not doing too badly for a hamster, Salem thought. To stay ahead of the cats, Stoney's tiny legs had to go at least four times as fast as theirs.

Which had to mean Stonehenge was getting *tired* four times as fast, too.

Stonehenge crossed the street and headed straight for a crowd of women dressed in long black robes. Nuns. Looking through a stack of paperbacks on a table in front of a used-book store. Salem

3 1

wondered if Stonehenge was going to make them part of the escape plan.

One of them spotted him and shrieked *"RATTO!"*—Italian for "RAT!" All of a sudden it looked like a dance contest. Salem was impressed. He'd seen a lot of nuns since they'd arrived in Rome. But this was the first time he'd seen any do the jitterbug.

A man with a broom went after Stonehenge ice-hockey style, with the hamster as the puck.

Two boys scrambled after him to see if they could capture Stonehenge barehanded, for a pet.

All of which made Stonehenge more difficult for the cats to follow.

He probably would have gotten away for good if it wasn't for a lucky slap shot by the man with the broom.

The blow caught Stonehenge by surprise. It knocked him off the sidewalk and into the cobblestone street just as a stream of bicycle racers zoomed past, barely missing him. When the cats jammed up momentarily for the bikes to pass, Salem noticed there were four of them now. At the restaurant there had been only two. They had picked up a couple of extra volunteers.

When the last of the bikes went by, Stonehenge made an emergency dive for the gutter, where a storm drain opened to a new escape route underground.

The other cats dived in after him. They went down as easily as letters in a mailbox. Except for Salem, who was more well fed than the street cats. For him, getting past the grate was a squeeze. When he finally did pop through, Salem was glad the drain shaft wasn't too deep and that the weather had been dry.

He found himself about four feet below street level, in a place where the shaft connected to a stone tunnel branching in two directions. Both ways were dark, and there was no way for Salem to tell which direction Stonehenge and the others had taken.

He listened hard, but the only sound he heard was his own heartbeat. *I guess they're gone forever,* he sighed. At least he'd tried.

Salem crouched to make the jump back to the drain cover. Suddenly, a split second before he sprang, he heard something and froze. There was a faint scratching noise in the distance.

It was the sound of claws tearing down the tunnel. Coming his way!

Two red dots flashed in the distance. Eyes! They were headed straight for Salem.

Stonehenge was back.

Salem blasted off . . .

And Stonehenge shot by beneath his feet.

His appearance had thrown Salem off a little bit. His front paws missed the drain cover and he fell back, just as the other cats came charging in.

Everybody crashed. It sounded like a five-violin pileup. Cats flew everywhere.

Stonehenge took advantage of the distraction. He made a U-turn and clambered over the wreckage and up the shaft back toward the street. Salem and the other cats were coming, too. They caught a glimpse of him disappearing around the grate.

Stoney's head start didn't last long. Two blocks later his path went past a fish market, where two new cats joined the chase. They were fresh and well rested. The only thing they were tired of was eating leftover seafood every night—hamster looked good.

Salem knew Stonehenge must be getting tired, because *he* was exhausted. The other cats were getting ahead of him.

A few blocks ahead the chase had already come to an end on a little *piazza*—Italian for "square" or "plaza," where Romans could sit or walk around away from traffic.

In the center of this piazza a fountain splashed. Along its edge were tall stone columns that had once supported a building. They were carved to look like women draped in long flowing robes.

Stonehenge had made the mistake of choosing one of the columns for an escape route. Now he was stranded at the top. Staring down at the water in the fountain, he wished he'd gone for a swim instead. Cats didn't do water. But it was too late for that. From where he was now, it looked way too far to jump.

As the cats from the restaurant and the street and the fish market gathered at the base of the column, the worried hamster checked the incoming streets for Salem.

But Salem was the *one* cat that was nowhere to be seen.

Chapter 5

Salem had heard stories about Saint Bernard dogs that rescued mountain climbers who got lost in the snow.

He'd read stories about horses that went home to their ranches to get help for their cowboys.

He'd even seen porpoises on TV that swam to rescue children who were involved in boating accidents.

But this had to be unique: the cat that risked its neck to save a hamster!

I'm just thankful this is taking place in a foreign country, Salem thought as he pounced from the red tile roof of a private residence on the piazza to the branches of a spreading tree in front.

Someplace where I won't be recognized or run into anyone I know, he thought as he leaped from the branches of the tree onto a streetlamp that overlooked the column by the fountain where the cats had treed Stonehenge.

I'd hate for a story like this to get back to Westbridge.

Salem shifted his paws on the big glass globe of the streetlamp, getting himself ready for the final leap to the column where Stonehenge was. If he could get there and Stonehenge could just hang on to him, Salem figured they could make it back the way he'd come, losing the cats from above.

Salem knew it could be done. It all depended on whether he and Stonehenge could keep their wits about them in a crisis. Keep their cool. Work as a team.

It'll never work, Salem thought. But he had to try. Without another thought he threw himself out of the tree toward Stoney's column.

38

Stonehenge turned just in time to *see* Salem. But not to *recognize* him. Instead, Stonehenge thought Salem was one of the other cats. So just as Salem landed, Stonehenge grabbed him by the ears and, rolling back, pulled Salem with him and kicked his hind legs into the cat's chest.

Something Gwen had taught him from self-defense class. A little judo.

Stonehenge had never tried it in real life, so he was amazed at how well it actually worked. Salem was surprised, too, as he found himself somersaulting over the water.

Except that Stonehenge had forgotten to let go at the end of the throw, so they were *both* going.

Together they plunged into the water.

About halfway back to the surface Stonehenge's eyes went wide with recognition.

"*S-Salem?!*" he bubbled.

"*Swim!*" Salem hissed when they broke the surface. *Of course it was me.* The two warlocks gave everything they had to putting some distance between themselves and the other cats.

It wasn't hard to do. The other cats were dumbfounded by what they'd just seen.

Their supper had been taken away by a cat that could fly.

Once he was sure they were out of danger, Salem stopped at a self-service laundry to dry off under a hot-air vent. Stonehenge, he noticed, was unusually quiet.

He wondered what was on Stonehenge's mind, but he didn't ask.

Stonehenge was trying to think of the right words to thank Salem for saving his life. But he wasn't having any luck.

It seemed like the only way Salem and Stonehenge could talk to each other was by quarreling.

"Well, I hate to break up the party, but we need to get back to Ristorante Bernini immediately, if not sooner," Salem said.

The tone in his voice made it clear that if Il Gatto and the locket were gone, Salem would put the blame on Stonehenge.

"I was just waiting for *you*, matey. It's this way, I believe," he said, heading for the street.

"You mean *this* way," Salem argued. "I don't think we want to go right back by your friends the cats."

Stonehenge scowled. It wasn't his fault they'd tried to eat him.

Salem marched off.

They were all the way back to Ristorante Bernini before either of them spoke again.

"He's gone!" they both exclaimed.

The only thing left at Il Gatto's table was the tip. They'd just missed him.

"I'd run away from home, if I could," Salem moaned. "But I'm already away from home. So that's out."

"Maybe we could find another enchanted locket," Stonehenge suggested.

"You know, like in a secondhand shop. An *enchanted* secondhand shop."

"You're really fishing," Salem said. "This is one particular enchanted locket. With one particular secret that only Sabrina is supposed to solve."

"I know, I know, but look, mate," Stonehenge said, sitting down on the curb. "A lot of witches and warlocks have tried to open that bloomin' locket, right? But for four hundred years, everyone's failed. How's a teenage witch like Sabrina supposed to figure it out in less than two weeks?"

"Sabrina can be quite clever when she's not worrying about which shoes to wear," Salem pointed out. "Especially for someone who's only half a witch. Just don't tell her I said that."

Stonehenge shook his head. "Face it, mate. She couldn't have opened it. In two weeks the magic would have been lost for good, anyway. That locket will become just another cheap souvenir. So it won't matter if we do the old switcheroo with a fake locket. She'd never find out."

Salem walked along a stone wall and looked up at the full moon. It was just rising over the Colosseum.

Stoney's idea was tempting.

But Salem knew Sabrina. She was no ordinary teenage witch. She was just wacky enough to figure the whole thing out.

He knew there was no other locket in the world like that one.

Not to mention the fact that Sabrina had this uncanny talent for knowing instantly when Salem was lying.

How could he go back without it?

Maybe I won't go back, he thought desperately as he walked along the stone wall. He'd read in Sabrina's guidebook that Rome was full of stray cats. Like the ones that had chased Stonehenge. Their ancestors had come from ancient Egypt. And the Romans had been feeding them ever since.

I'll run away and become a stray, he thought sadly. *Live in the streets. Like a poor little orphan cat . . .*

Suddenly he heard shouting.

Salem looked up. Bright lights blinded him. A man began to shout at him in Italian. Salem didn't know the words. But he thought they sounded angry.

Oh, no, Salem thought. *What have I done now?* "Stonehenge," he gasped, "what's he saying?"

"He's talking so fast, I'm not sure," Stonehenge whispered back. "But I think I heard 'Grab that cat!' "

Salem blinked into the glare as several pairs of hands reached out for him.

Chapter 6

A woman clutched Salem firmly in her arms.

Salem blinked against the bright lights that surrounded him.

"Pazzo gatto!" a man cried. His eyes were wild. He waved his arms dramatically as if he were in great agony.

Crazy cat? Salem thought. *Ha!* The man was the one who looked crazy.

But then the man stopped. He whirled and stared at Salem. A hush fell across the street. Without speaking a word, the man studied Salem from the tops of his ears to the tip of his tail. He paced back and forth, muttering to himself. And then he stopped and began to laugh. *"Perfetto!"* he cried, then began shouting orders to the others standing around.

The woman sat down in a chair and began to brush Salem's black fur. Stonehenge scurried up behind them.

"Stonehenge," Salem asked, "what's going on? Who is that man?"

"Don't you know anything?" Stonehenge said. "That's Visione—one of Italy's most famous movie directors! We wandered onto his set while they were shooting!"

"No wonder he was so upset," Salem whispered nervously.

"Not anymore," Stonehenge explained. "He thinks your sad, hopeless look of guilt and remorse is perfect to convey the sad, hopeless mood of the scene he's shooting for his new movie, *L'Amore Perduto tra le Rovine*—or *'Love Lost Among the Ruins.'*"

Salem gasped. "You mean—I'm going to be in an Italian film? What do they want me to do?"

"Just what you did already," Stonehenge whispered. "Walk along the wall and look sad and hopeless."

"I can do that!" Salem whispered back. *Especially if it will make me a movie star.*

Salem closed his eyes as the woman carried him to the set. He tried to get into character. It was hard to feel sad and hopeless—because he was so excited!

Think of the locket, Salem reminded himself. *Just imagine what Sabrina, Zelda, Hilda, and Edward will do to you when they find out it's gone!*

That did the trick.

Salem wandered along the wall looking sad and hopeless, a stray kitty lost in the arms of the Roman night. He weaved around the legs of the main actress. He looked up at her with longing. Tears filled his eyes. *Am I good or what?* he thought proudly.

With a sob, the actress scooped him up and hugged him to her cheek.

47

"Cut!" the director called in Italian.

The actress instantly went from tears to laughter. *"Grazie, bello gatto!"* she cried, and gave him a great big kiss.

Salem started to purr, but his voice cracked. Kissed by the most beautiful actress in all of Rome. And she called him a handsome cat! *Darn! How come you never have a camera when you need one?*

Suddenly he heard applause and cheers. Salem had fans! He smiled and purred at the crowd of Romans and tourists who had gathered to watch.

Among them was a face he recognized.

Il Gatto—the thief!

Salem's heart lurched. "Stonehenge—look!"

Salem pointed a paw toward the thief, who stood now with an attractive girl with long dark hair. She looked as if she was only a couple of years older than Sabrina.

"That must be his girlfriend," Stonehenge said.

"Maybe that's the 'someone' he told the waiter he had to meet," Salem said. "Someone should warn her he's a crook!"

The movie crew began to pack up, and the crowd broke up to wander their separate ways.

Salem sighed. His career in movies had been short but sweet!

Especially sweet was the fact that Salem and Stonehenge were back on Il Gatto's trail. Quickly they followed him and his girl, hoping for another chance at the locket.

After a short walk the couple sat down on a bench near a little park. Salem and Stonehenge hid in the bushes where the hamster could listen and translate. "I can't quite catch it all, mate," he reported. "But I think he's about to give the girl the locket as a present!"

There was only one thing to do!

Salem licked his paw and slicked back a stray bit of fur.

Then he scooted onto the sidewalk and sauntered up to the girl, turning on the charm. He purred and begged for a pat on the head.

"Ah, bello gatto!" she exclaimed, breaking away from the thief. She picked up Salem and began to give him all her attention.

The look on Il Gatto's face told Salem he'd ruined the mood. Good. Now maybe he could manage to . . .

Too late. The locket went back into Il Gatto's pocket as he jumped to his feet and hailed a cab. Then he grabbed his girl by the hand and pulled her playfully toward the curb. Salem fell from her lap.

"How rude!" Salem exclaimed.

But he didn't have time to ponder the manners of thieves. Because just then the taxi pulled away from the curb!

"Come on, Stonehenge, run!" Salem cried.

"I can't," Stonehenge said. "I'm too

worn out from being chased by the cats. You'll have to go on without me."

Salem groaned. He couldn't leave Stonehenge behind. The little rodent might never find his way home to Gwen. He'd spent a lot of time and energy already to save him.

But now Il Gatto was getting away—again!

Chapter 7

Salem figured out what to do.

The cab driver screeched to a stop to scream out his window at a pedestrian. "Stonehenge, hang on to my tail!" Salem cried. Then he leaped on top of the sleek yellow taxi!

"Salem!" Stonehenge squeaked. "What are we doing?"

"It's called a free ride," Salem called. "Hang on!"

Salem locked his claws onto the small lighted TAXI sign on the car's roof.

"Salem!" Stonehenge cried as the taxi jolted forward. "This is the stupidest idea you've had yet!"

The taxi driver drove like a maniac.

Brightly painted Vespas—small motor-bikes—zipped in and around the cars. Pedestrians darted in front of them across the busy streets. All the stoplights in Rome had switched to flashing yellow for the night—every man for himself!

It was terrifying—and exhilarating. Salem couldn't help but enjoy the wind in his fur. The view of the city sights by night. If only he wasn't holding on for dear life with a hamster pinching his tail!

At last they swerved to the curb. Il Gatto and his girlfriend stepped out and strolled toward an outdoor movie theater where a show was about to begin.

Salem and Stonehenge hurried after them. They peeked over the wall and watched as the couple sat down in a center row.

Then Il Gatto turned to the girl. And smiled. And pulled something from his pocket. The locket. He showed it to her.

The girl gasped in surprise and delight.

When he hooked it around her neck, she gave him a kiss.

Then the outdoor lights dimmed. And Salem and Stonehenge crawled under the seats and made their way toward the happy couple.

Salem stopped at the pointy black shoes he recognized as Il Gatto's. He motioned for Stonehenge to keep down.

At the next pair over, he bravely looked up from under the seat and smiled.

The girl fell for it, hook, line, and sinker.

"Mio piccolo amico!" she cried ("My little friend," Stonehenge translated). She scooped Salem up into her lap.

She turned to Il Gatto and said something, and Il Gatto frowned.

"She's teasing him because Il Gatto—the cat burglar—hates cats!" Stonehenge whispered from under the seat.

"I knew this guy had no heart," Salem sniffed.

"But now," Stonehenge went on, "she's

telling him she wants to keep you and take you home."

"I might like that," Salem muttered, "if she breaks up with *him.*"

Salem playfully batted the locket that hung around the girl's neck. She laughed. Il Gatto glared. He probably expected to get all the girl's attention after he gave her the locket. Not share it with a stray cat!

When the movie started, the girl removed the locket and held it out for Salem to play with. Il Gatto protested. But the girl just laughed and turned her attention to the movie screen.

Salem held his breath. *Everything's going exactly according to plan*, he thought.

Salem waited until Il Gatto and his girlfriend were lost in the movie. Then he casually slipped the locket down to Stonehenge beneath the seats.

BANG! A shot went off. It was in the movie—

But it startled the girl, and Salem jumped away with the locket and Stonehenge in tow. Il Gatto dived under the seat, trying to catch him. *"Tu gatto!"* he cried.

"Ratto?!" a lady two rows back cried. She thought he said "rat."

"Ratto?" someone else shouted.

"Ratto! Ratto! Ratto!" people started screaming.

Everyone panicked. People leaped from their seats.

Then one lady spotted Stonehenge. *"Il ratto!"* she cried, and swatted at him with her purse.

Salem pulled him away just in time.

"Saving your fur is becoming quite a habit," Salem complained as he and Stonehenge escaped into the street.

After a few blocks they stopped to catch their breath.

"I think we got away," Salem said, daring to hope. He laid his paw protectively on the golden necklace. "With the locket, this time!"

"Now all we have to do is find our way home," Stonehenge said. He looked both ways along the dark and narrow street.

Salem had no idea where they were either. "Yes, that is a problem, isn't it?"

Chapter 8

"Hello?" said a woman's voice on the phone. Salem was delighted to hear her American accent.

Before answering, he quickly double-checked the area for people. He didn't want anyone to see him using the bright orange pay phone to call the U.S. embassy. You weren't supposed to do that if you were a *cat*.

"Well, hello!" Salem said when he was sure the coast was clear. "Let me begin by saying it's nice to talk to a fellow American!"

Stonehenge rolled his eyes.

"How can I help you?" said the woman at the embassy. They got calls from American tourists in Rome every day. Sometimes it was about a serious problem, but most of the calls were about ordinary things. Things that could be looked up in a guidebook.

Like Salem's request for directions back to his hotel.

"Ordinarily I'd take a taxi, but I'm a little short of cash," Salem fibbed.

Luckily for him, Rome was a city of fountains. And it was a tradition for tourists to throw coins into the fountains while making wishes. Salem had managed to "borrow" a few coins for the pay phone by fishing them out of the water. He read the woman the name of the street they were on off the corner sign, gave her their hotel's name, and then listened to the sound of paper crinkling as she checked a map.

A few minutes later Salem hung up the phone. "See?" he said. "It's very simple."

59

Stonehenge frowned. Salem always acted like he knew everything.

"Now, if you'll just give me a minute to adjust this locket, we'll be on our way," Salem said. He fumbled with the chain, trying to double it up so it would fit his neck. Stonehenge was the one with the agile fingers, but Salem refused to let the hamster help. Stonehenge was getting the message that Salem didn't need or want any assistance from him.

Finally Salem got the locket adjusted and onto his neck so that it wouldn't drag on the ground. "Follow me," he said, and headed down the street. Stonehenge took up the rear.

Little did they know that every move they made was being closely watched.

Chapter 9

Out of the shadows stepped an old man and a young boy. Their movements were quick and confident, especially the old man's. With a single sweep of his arm he scooped Salem into a heavy cloth bag, closed it with a twist, and returned to the shadows. It was over in the blink of an eye.

Salem struggled in vain against the bag. He couldn't punch out, and the fabric was too heavy to get his claws through and tear. After a few tries he decided to save his strength.

Instead of fighting, he listened. To his captor's boots on a cobblestone street. To the groan of the wobbly metal staircase they took to a second floor. To the secret

knock on a metal door and the squeak as it opened and the groan as it shut behind them.

A man wearing heavy-soled shoes crossed the room and took the bag. He spoke in Italian to the others, then laid the bag on a table. Holding Salem through the cloth by the scruff of the neck, he rolled back the opening to take a look at the locket and his collar and the tag Signora Guadagno had put on him when Sabrina checked in. Then the man again said something in Italian to the ones who had captured Salem.

As long as his head was out of the bag, Salem checked out the room. It looked like the storage room for an antiques store—no windows, bad lighting, but lots and lots of high-quality stuff all around.

The bag man and the kid dragged over a large birdcage—Victorian style with a domed top and flattened-paw feet, dating from about 1920, Salem decided—and they pushed him inside. Why didn't they just yank off the locket and let him go?

A motor whirred and a gate clattered behind a heavy steel door in the wall. A man in a broad-brimmed black hat pushed it open from the other side and rolled an antique side table into the room on a hand truck. Salem gave it a sharp look.

Marble top, gilt-and-plaster legs, and a forty-inch mirror, he reckoned. *In good condition, that little gem should fetch around six grand—not bad!*

The man with the heavy-soled shoes settled into a chair at another table and opened a metal box of paper money. The man who had carted in the antique sat down, too, and removed his hat.

Salem's eyes went wide.

It was Il Gatto!

Salem didn't need to speak Italian to understand what was going on. These men were crooks. The antiques in this room were stolen.

63

Oh, great, Salem thought. He couldn't *wait* for Il Gatto to see him with his girl-friend's locket.

Something moved next to the claw foot of a Queen Anne high-backed chair in the corner, and Salem's eyes went to it instinctively. He watched it scurry behind a rosewood three-drawer chest with brass pulls and come out over the top of a walnut Chippendale slant-front desk circa 1760. *Try not to scratch it,* he thought. From there it was just a short hop to the shell tray around the base of Salem's cage. For once Salem was glad to see it was Stonehenge.

"I tracked you all the way from the street," Stonehenge whispered between the bars of Salem's cage. "Do you know how difficult it was to talk my way in here past the rats? You were *kidnapped* back there!"

"Very good," Salem said. "To compete for our grand prize, now tell me how you're going to *open this cage.*"

"Let me finish," Stonehenge complained. "The man and the boy tried to sell your locket to the boss over there. But he thinks they can get more by holding you for ransom—any cat owner who would give their cat a locket like that . . ."

"I get the picture," Salem griped. "Unfortunately, Sabrina's allowance won't go very far."

"Blimey! I was just about to say that!" Stonehenge snapped, then took a deep breath and calmed down again. "So in other words, you're in a great deal of *danger*. I felt it was important to point that out."

"In case you haven't noticed, our old friend Il Gatto happens to be seated over there, too, Stonehenge. I think I know that if you don't open this cage, I'm basically toast."

"Right," Stonehenge said. "I'm glad we see eye to eye on that. I also want to point out that you're going to be all right."

65

"Open the cage?"

"Because I am here to save you."

Salem flinched.

"And by saving you now, I am paying you back for any part I may have played in the temporary loss of Sabrina's locket."

Salem gulped. "Agreed."

"This also pays you back for saving me from the other cats."

"Agreed."

"And . . ." Stonehenge's voice cracked. "I also want to say . . . that I'm sorry. Sorry that I caused you any trouble, Salem. And I'm grateful. Grateful to you—for saving my life back there."

Something was forming in Salem's eye. "Stonehenge, Stonehenge, Stonehenge," he said. "I'm sorry, too. Sorry for the things I said. I think you're . . . I think you're . . . I think you're . . ."

Stonehenge looked up at Salem.

But before Salem could finish what he was saying, some chairs dragged across the floor—Il Gatto and the boss were getting up from the table. Salem and Stonehenge were out of time.

"Open this cage, you little rodent!" Salem hissed.

Stonehenge stuck out his tongue and gave Salem the raspberry. For a minute Salem thought Stonehenge wasn't going to help him. But then the hamster turned the latch and threw open the door.

Together, they hit the ground running.

The men yelled, *"Arresto!"*

Salem scatted after Stonehenge alongside a matched pair of Napoleon III chairs. They were in such good condition that Salem would have stopped to admire them had Stonehenge not dragged him along by the ear.

"Come on!" Stonehenge squeaked over his shoulder. "I left a window cracked for you behind that Federal-style mahogany

three-drawer sideboard! From there, we can take the fire escape to the street!"

"Magnificent!" Salem said.

"Thank you!" said Stonehenge.

"I meant the sideboard!" said Salem.

Chapter 10

First they went down the fire escape.

Then they went up the street.

They passed the outdoor theater where Il Gatto and his girlfriend had gone to the movies.

They went around the fountain with the columns that looked like women in robes.

They went by the Colosseum, where they had been in the movie.

They passed the used bookstore where Stonehenge had frightened the nuns.

They went down the alley and banged alongside the trash cans.

They went past the restaurant where Il Gatto had had dinner.

Then, just to make sure they weren't still being followed, they took the long way back.

Past a famous church called the Santa Maria in Cosmedin. "There's something in there I want you to see," Stonehenge told Salem. "It'll only take a minute."

Set into the wall of the church was a huge stone carving of a bearded face. "It's called the *Bocca della Verità*," Stonehenge said. "Mouth of Truth."

"Very interesting," Salem said. It looked like a big drain-hole cover to him.

"It was probably made as a big drain-hole cover," Stonehenge went on. "But now there is a legend attached. It is said that if you put your hand into the mouth, you *must* tell the truth."

"Or?" Salem said.

"Try it," Stonehenge said.

Salem put his paw into the mouth of the carving.

"Back there while you were in the bird-cage," Stonehenge said, "what was it you were saying? Before you got interrupted."

Salem tried to think. "I remember," he said. "I think I was saying . . . uh . . ."

"According to the legend, if you don't tell the truth, the *Bocca della Verità* will bite off your hand!"

"Er, I assume that applies to *paws* as well?"

Stonehenge nodded.

Salem looked at his paw in the mouth of the carving. Then he looked at Stonehenge. Then he looked back at his paw. Then he looked at Stonehenge again.

"Go on," Stonehenge said.

"I think I wanted to say that I thought you were all right, Stonehenge. That maybe I kind of like you." Salem admitted.

And the *Bocca della Verità* did *not* bite off Salem's paw.

71

Chapter 11

Salem knew they still faced a frightening challenge.

They had escaped the *bad* guys. But not the *good* guys.

Sabrina and Gwen!

"What time is it?" Salem asked Stonehenge as they plodded up the street toward Signora Guadagno's small hotel.

"Time for any last requests," Stonehenge replied.

Salem searched the sky for stars. He needed to find a good one to make a wish on. A wish that Sabrina, Gwen, and Alberto were having a really good time. So good a time that they weren't home yet.

When they got back to their hotel, Salem

stopped across the street. He and Stonehenge looked up to the second floor. The windows were dark.

"Thank goodness," Stonehenge gasped. "That means they're not back yet."

"Or," Salem worried, "it means they came back hours ago, and already went to bed."

"Then we'll just have to sneak in without waking 'em, mate," Stonehenge suggested. And with that he scampered across the quiet, dark street.

Salem sighed, and followed. They'd had a lot of good luck already that night. He wasn't sure if there was any left.

Carefully and quietly they padded through the gate, across the courtyard, and up the stairs.

Just in case, Salem removed the locket and hid it in a planter at the bottom of the staircase. He wanted to hide the evidence until he was sure the coast was clear. Then he'd come back for the locket.

Together the two animals crept quietly up the stairs.

But when they reached their room, a huge shadow loomed in the opened doorway.

And it wasn't Sabrina or Gwen.

"Ooops," Salem whispered. "We forgot somebody."

They had to get past Signora Guadagno.

"Buona sera," Signora Guadagno said without a smile.

Good evening? Salem thought. *Not hardly!*

"Would you two like to tell me where you've been?" she asked. "And," she added, folding her arms across her ample chest, "who left the shower running?"

Salem made a big show of shivering. "Eeww! You know how we cats hate water!"

Signora Guadagno snorted. "Well, you might as well come in," she said. She held open the door, and the two animals skittered inside. Was she angry at them? Enough to tell Sabrina and Gwen?

Salem set one paw inside the room, then froze. He sniffed the air. He couldn't believe his nose.

"Pizza?" he exclaimed.

Signora Guadagno shrugged. "The man he comes with the pizza. I figure you had to go out. I pay him."

Salem flipped open the pizza box, and his stomach growled in eager delight. "I—" His voice broke. He couldn't remember when he'd been so hungry. "*Grazie*, signora," he said with tears in his eyes. He took a big bite. It was no longer hot. But for once Salem was too hungry to complain.

"Ah! *Mama mia!*" Signora Guadagno exclaimed, picking up a slice. "The pizza—it's cold!"

"No, it's fine, really—!" Salem said. He tried to snag a slice before she whisked the pizza box away.

"It is a crime to eat cold pizza," Signora Guadagno declared. "Come! I will heat it up for you."

"Uh, we'll be right down!" Salem called after her. "We just want to, um, uh—"

"Wash our paws?" Stonehenge finished for his friend.

As soon as Signora Guadagno had disappeared to go to her kitchen, Salem raced down the stairs. He grabbed the locket, then darted back into their room.

The mattress on Sabrina's bed was so heavy! But at last Salem managed to squeeze his paw in and leave the enchanted locket where Sabrina had originally hidden it.

Only then did he feel truly safe.

"We did it, Stonehenge," Salem gasped. "Give me some paw!"

Unfortunately, his high five–style slap sent the tiny hamster flying backward across the room.

"Stonehenge!" Salem cried as he ran to

check his furry little friend. "Are you all right?"

"Fine, mate," Stonehenge replied with a smile. "In fact, I don't know when I've had a better time."

Salem smiled. "I hate to admit it," he said. "But me, too, little buddy; me, too. Not counting my B.C. years, of course."

"B.C. years?"

"Before Cat," Salem clarified as together they followed the smell of pizza to Signora Guadagno's kitchen.

"Perfetto!" Signora Guadagno announced, and set the pizza box down on the floor.

"Perfect!" Salem agreed as he and Stonehenge pounced on the perfect pie. *Hey, I'm actually beginning to pick up a little Italian*, he realized. Maybe it would come in handy the next time he tried to get into an Italian restaurant back home.

Salem licked his paws. "Signora Guadagno, you have a heart of gold."

"I know," she said. "And speaking of gold, you owe me for the pizza."

Salem gulped. "Uh, well, I'm a little short of cash right now. How about you, Stonehenge?"

Stonhenge shook his head. "I'm broke, mate."

Signora Guadagno shrugged and stood up. "Ah, *no problema*," she said. "So you two can do a little work to pay me back."

She led the two animals to a huge pile of dishes.

"A *little* work?" Salem muttered. But then he shrugged. *Oh, well, if this is the price I have to pay for the night I just had—it's worth it!*

Minutes after Salem and Stonehenge trudged up to their room, exhausted from their adventures, they heard footsteps on the stairs.

Giggling told them that Sabrina, Gwen, and Alberto had come home at last.

"Quick, Stonehenge," Salem whispered. "Pretend to be asleep."

"It won't be hard, mate," Stonehenge said. "I can hardly keep my eyes open."

Stonehenge dashed to his cage and burrowed into the wood chips. Salem left a small table light on. Then he curled up at the foot of Sabrina's bed just as the door to the room creaked open.

"Good night," Alberto called to the girls. "It was very good to see me."

"Yes," Sabrina laughed. "It was good to see *you*, too! We had fun!"

Then the girls hurried into the room.

"Shhh!" Sabrina whispered, tiptoeing toward her bed. "Look! Salem and Stonehenge are asleep. Aren't they cute?"

Stonehenge snorted in his cage. Salem squeezed his eyes shut tight and hoped the girls didn't notice.

Sabrina sat down on the edge of the bed. "Oh, bother!" she said, using Gwen's pet

79

word. "I forgot to bring Salem a doggie bag from the restaurant."

"Doggie bag?" Gwen said. "Allow me."

"Uh, no, Gwen, wait—!"

Gwen snapped her fingers.

A doghouse appeared.

"Bother!" Gwen complained.

Salem tried not to giggle. Gwen was still struggling with her magic.

"Oh, happens to me all the time," Sabrina said politely. She snapped her fingers, and the doghouse went away.

"Now, let me see," Sabrina said. "I wonder what his favorite Italian dish is . . ."

Salem turned over, as if in his sleep. "Lasagne . . ." he whispered. "Lasagne . . ."

Gwen giggled. "He even dreams about food?"

"That's my Salem," Sabrina said with a grin.

"Grant his wish . . .
An Italian dish!"

8 0

A steaming plate of cheesy homemade lasagne appeared on the table.

"Salem," Sabrina whispered, shaking the cat gently on the shoulder. "Wake up."

"Come on, Stonehenge," Gwen called to her hamster. "You, too."

Salem twisted and turned. He sniffed the air, and slowly opened his eyes. He yawned, then pretended to spot the plate of food for the first time. "It's my dream come true!" he gushed. "Lasagne—for me? Oh, Sabrina, you are such a dear."

"Well, we felt sorry for you two," Sabrina said.

"Sorry for us?" Salem asked as he dug into the lasagne.

"For being stuck in the room all night," Sabrina said. "With nothing to do."

Salem gulped, then swallowed the big lump in his throat.

He and Stonehenge exchanged a guilty look.

Maybe one day, Salem thought, *if Sabrina solves the secret of the locket . . .*

Maybe one day—if Sabrina is in a REALLY good mood—

I'll tell her about tonight.

But not right now.

"Did you have a good time?" he asked her instead.

"Awesome," Sabrina said. "We had a fabulous dinner. And we saw a movie at an outdoor arena under the stars."

Salem nearly choked. Sabrina had to pound him on the back.

"Er, really?" Salem asked.

"Halfway through the show there was some kind of commotion down front," Gwen reported. "Somebody saw a rat or something. But other than that, it was a lovely way to spend the evening."

Salem ate another bite of lasagne and tried to look innocent.

Stonehenge crept over beside Salem

and nibbled a bit of cheese. "Salem," he whispered into the black cat's ear. "How can you eat all this lasagne after the pizza you just inhaled in Signora Guadagno's kitchen?"

Salem shrugged. "It would look suspicious if I didn't," he whispered back. "They think we've been stuck up here with two bowls of pet chow. Besides, I'm starving. I burned a lot of extra calories running around Rome tonight trying to repair your mistakes."

"*My* mistakes?" Stonehenge exclaimed, his voice rising. "What about you? Why, you were the one who—"

"What are they arguing about now?" Gwen asked as she and Sabrina stepped out on the balcony.

"Who knows?" Sabrina said with a sigh. "I guess it's too much to ask to expect a cat and a hamster to get along."

"I guess you're right." Gwen smiled at

83

Sabrina. "Too bad they can't be friends like us, eh?"

The girls leaned on the railing, enjoying the starry night, still too excited to go to sleep.

They missed seeing Salem lay a friendly paw on Stoney's shoulder. "So," he asked his hamster friend, "what do you think we should do *tomorrow* night?"

Epilogue

Six months later

Salem!" Aunt Zelda called as she came in the front door of the Spellmans' Victorian home in Westbridge, Massachusetts. She held up a handful of mail. "You got another postcard from your friend Stonehenge." She handed it to Salem on the couch. He was eating dinner with Sabrina in front of the TV.

"Pasta—again?" Hilda asked.

"Hey, the Italians eat it almost every meal," Sabrina said.

"I'll have you know there are more than thirty kinds of pasta," Salem reported.

"And hundreds of sauces. Why, we've only just begun the tour!"

"I can't believe our Salem is getting mail from a hamster," Zelda whispered to her younger sister.

"What does Stonehenge have to say?" Sabrina asked.

" 'Greetings from Iceland,' " Salem read. " 'Wish you were here.' "

"Iceland—again?" Sabrina said. She had a feeling *that* trip was the result of mixed-up magic! "Poor Gwen. She really needs a tutor!"

Just then a commercial came on for a new movie coming to the artsy theater in Westbridge. "Hey, look, Salem. Maybe we should go see this!" Sabrina exclaimed. "It's an Italian movie, filmed in Rome. We might see some of the sights we remember from our trip."

Salem got goose bumps as he leaned toward the TV. *Could it be . . . ?*

A scene from the movie showed a beautiful young Italian woman on a Roman street at night as a stray black cat wandered up to her. Sobbing, she picked up the cat and hugged him tight.

Sabrina laughed. "Salem, that cat looks just like you."

"Heh, heh," Salem said.

Sabrina leaned forward and stared at the TV. "A *lot* like you."

"Ridiculous," Salem replied.

"Salem," Sabrina said with a suspicious frown, "*why* does that cat look *exactly* like you?"

But Salem just shrugged. He couldn't answer. It wouldn't be polite, after all. His mouth was full of pasta.

Should I tell her? he wondered.

Nah, not tonight.

He gazed at himself as the camera zoomed in for a closeup. My, my, he *did* look fantastic. When the movie came out on video, he'd have to get copies for *all* his friends.

Cat Care Tips

Unlike Salem, in general most cats do not like to travel or be in new environments. They tend to be most comfortable in their own homes and should not be taken places unless necessary. Some cats will adapt easily to a new environment while others may be frightened and hide for many days.

#1 If your cat is having a hard time adjusting to a new environment, you should keep him or her in one room with the litter and food until he or she becomes more comfortable and decides to explore.

#2 Spend lots of time with your cat in the new environment and make sure he or she is eating well.

#3 Do not let cats outside in a new environment until you are sure they are comfortable and know how to find the way home (to the new place). You should be with your cat the first couple of times that he or she goes outside in a new environment.

About the Authors

Cathy East Dubowski and Mark Dubowski have written many books separately and together, including books in the *Sabrina the Teenage Witch*, *Salem's Tails*, *The Secret World of Alex Mack*, and *The Mystery Files of Shelby Woo* series. Their book for younger readers, *Cave Boy*, which Mark also illustrated, is an International Reading Association Children's Choice. The Dubowskis live in Chapel Hill, North Carolina.

BRAND-NEW SERIES!

Meet up with suspense and mystery in

FRANK AND JOE HARDY: THE CLUES BROTHERS™

▼

#1 The Gross Ghost Mystery

#2 The Karate Clue

#3 First Day, Worst Day

#4 Jump Shot Detectives

#5 Dinosaur Disaster

#6 Who Took the Book?

#7 The Abracadabra Case

#8 The Doggone Detectives

By Franklin W. Dixon

Look for a brand-new story every other month
at your local bookseller

A MINSTREL BOOK

Published by Pocket Books   1398-05

Do your younger brothers and sisters want to read books like yours?

Let them know there are books just for *them!*

They can join Nancy Drew and her best friends as they collect clues and solve mysteries in

THE NANCY DREW NOTEBOOKS®

Starting with

#1 The Slumber Party Secret

#2 The Lost Locket

#3 The Secret Santa

#4 Bad Day for Ballet

AND

Meet up with suspense and mystery in Frank and Joe Hardy:

The Clues Brothers™

Starting with

#1 The Gross Ghost Mystery

#2 The Karate Clue

#3 First Day, Worst Day

#4 Jump Shot Detectives

Look for a brand-new story every other month at your local bookseller

 A MINSTREL® BOOK

Published by Pocket Books   1366-02

Todd Strasser's
AGAINST THE ODDS™

Shark Bite
The sailboat is sinking, and Ian just saw the
biggest shark of his life.

Grizzly Attack
They're trapped in the Alaskan wilderness
with no way out.

Buzzard's Feast
Danger in the desert!

Gator Prey
They know the gators are coming for
them...it's only a matter of time.

Published by Pocket Books

2023